Also by Per Petterson

Ashes in My Mouth, Sand in My Shoes

Per Petterson

Translated from the Norwegian
by Don Bartlett

Harvill *Secker*
LONDON

Published by Harvill Secker 2013

9 8 7 6 5 4 3 2 1

Copyright © Forlaget Oktober, Oslo 1987
English translation copyright © Don Bartlett 2013

Per Petterson has asserted his right under the
Copyright, Designs and Patents Act 1988 to
be identified as the author of this work

First published with the title *Ekko Runnen, sana i skon* in
1987 by Forlaget Oktober, Oslo

First published in Great Britain in 2013 by
Harvill Secker
Random House
20 Vauxhall Bridge Road
London SW1V 2SA

www.vintage-books.co.uk

Addresses for companies within The Random House Group
Limited can be found at:
www.randomhouse.co.uk/offices.htm

The Random House Group Limited Reg. No. 954009

A CIP catalogue record for this book is available
from the British Library

ISBN 9781846553707

This book was published with the financial
assistance of NORLA

Contents

To my father, Arthur Petterson, 1911–1990

A Man Without Shoes

Dad had a face that Arvid loved to watch, and at the same time made him nervous as it wasn't just a face but also a rock in the forest with its furrows and hollows, at least if he squinted when he looked. Of course you can be a bit unsettled if you look at your dad and suddenly there is a large rock where his head used to be.

Those who liked to comment on this kind of thing said that the two of them looked a lot like each other and that was perhaps what made Arvid most nervous, but when he glanced in the mirror he didn't understand what they meant for Dad was blond, and all Arvid saw in the mirror was two round cheeks and plainly Dad did not have them.

But most of the time Dad was just Dad, some-one that Arvid liked and dared to touch. Uncle Rolf said that Dad's face had a determination that couldn't determine where to go, but Uncle Rolf had always been a big mouth.

Dad worked in a shoe factory and had gone up through the ranks at Salomon Shoes at Kiellands Square. He was a skilled worker now and had just become a foreman when the Norwegian shoe industry capsized and sank like the *Titanic*. After that he moved from factory to factory, as if they were ice floes in the Bunne Fjord in spring, further and further away, and in the end he found a job on the island of Fyn in Denmark. It was a responsible post for a worker, in the office for half the week, recognition, Mum said, let's be clear about that, and she seemed to like the thought of returning to the old country.

He was away for six months, and Arvid and Gry and Mum tiptoed around waiting for the signal to follow. Arvid had slowly begun to say goodbye to the things around him: his room with the model planes hanging from the ceiling, the bullfinch tree down by the dustbin and the secret path beneath the bushes on the Slope. But then one evening Dad was standing in the hall with a crumpled smile and a large suitcase in his hand and he said:

'Sorry, folks, but I've never been much of a paper pusher.'

He'd had a pint or two, and Arvid could see that straight away.

They were all so bewildered they never got round to asking about anything except what was in the suitcase. When it turned out it was full of marzipan and whisky and Toblerone and Elephant beer from the duty-free shop on the Danish ferry, they crowded into the kitchen like a pack of hungry pups. It was a small kitchen, so the children had to stand while the adults sat around the table with a dram to consider the situation in an adult way. And of course Uncle Rolf had to have his say. It was a mystery to Arvid why he came round so often, didn't he have his own place to live?

'The thing is, Frank, you don't have any social aspirations, and you know it!' said Uncle Rolf, and the kitchen went so quiet you could hear the rain on the windowpanes. It was such a quiet, sneaky pitter-patter that no one had heard it until then. Outside, it was November and dark, the night was full of nasty naked trees scraping against the walls just like in *Captain Miki and the Man with the Evil Eye*. Arvid stood with his backside against the sink in the kitchen, where just now it had been so cosy. He had a half-eaten Tom's marzipan log in his hand and hardly dared sniffle, even though he had a bad cold.

No one in the kitchen really knew what 'social aspirations' meant, it had to be a new expression, but Uncle Rolf had read a few books and thought he was damn clever. Anyway, it was not a compliment, Arvid could see the irritation crawling around his dad's face, and it was contagious for he could feel himself getting upset.

'*Skål*, Rolf, and let's hope the social aspirations don't swell your head as you've got so many of them,' Dad said, and his eyes were narrow and tired too, when he knocked back what was left in his glass. And then he got up and went to bed.

Uncle Rolf sat twirling his glass between his fingers, but no one talked to him any more, and Mum began to wipe the table, so he drank up and went home to his flat in Vålerenga. The flat was full of clutter and dust balls everywhere, and *Allers* and *Reader's Digest* and *Norsk Ukeblad* strewn across the coffee table, and whenever Arvid came to visit him he had to help with the dishes even though he never did that at home. Uncle Rolf didn't have a wife, and who would want his sort, Arvid said to himself.

Uncle Rolf worked at the Jordan brush factory in Økern. There he stood at a machine all day making sure the bristles were properly inserted into the holes of the red, green and blue toothbrushes. Such a waste of time, Arvid thought, making toothbrushes, day in, day out.

But two weeks after Dad returned home from Denmark, he was standing at his own machine, next to Uncle Rolf's. Uncle Rolf had got him the job. It was unbearable.

And on top of that Uncle Rolf liked his job,

even though he was always reading the *Reader's Digest* and that sort of magazine and telling them how he was going to start up his own business: patents, imports and rubbish like that. He liked talking, there was nothing he loved more than the sound of his own voice when he was speaking about all the things he was going to do. And though Arvid was so small that no one thought he understood a thing, he did understand that Uncle Rolf would be making toothbrushes for the rest of his life. Not that he talked that much about toothbrushes, everyone must have known that there were limits to how much you could say about something as stupid as toothbrushes.

Shoes, on the other hand, there was a lot to say about them. Gym shoes, smart shoes, ladies' shoes, children's shoes, ski boots, riding boots. Dad talked a lot about shoes, and he knew what he was talking about. But now it was over. Now you couldn't even say the word 'sole' aloud. If you did Dad would lose his temper.

'In this house we *wear* shoes, we don't talk about them, is that clear!' he said, and then there was silence, although Arvid could easily see that his mother was annoyed by all the detours they had to take.

Downstairs in his cellar room the piles of toothbrushes were mounting up. They were the seconds that Dad had been given at work, with handles that were too short or bristles missing. Soon they would have enough toothbrushes to last them into the next life, if such a thing existed, but Dad didn't believe that and neither did Mum. Arvid was not so sure, because Gran in Denmark said something different and she ought to know. She went to church every Sunday, and she composed hymns.

Arvid hated those toothbrushes inside their plastic bags, sorted by colour. They took up space and were pushing the shoe samples out of the closet, and the rolls of leather and the lasts and the shoemaking tools Dad used to repair their shoes with when the toes were yawning or a heel fell off. Arvid used to sit on a stool watching, and there was the good smell of leather and his dad's back, that was fine to look at when he was working.

'What are you doing now, Dad?'

'I'm experimenting,' they might say to each other, and Dad did that a lot, spent time pondering all sorts of problems that there must have been with shoes.

Now that too was over. And one day Arvid saw his dad carrying out the rolls of leather and the shoe samples and stuffing them into the dustbin by the bullfinch tree. Then he was back down in the cellar, and there was a terrible pounding on the stairs, and after a while he came up, panting, with a huge basket of shoe lasts, lasts of all sizes, elegant and shiny with their varnish, and they had been such a wonderful sight on the shelf in the lumber room, where they used to be, and they seemed to be dancing.

Dad put down the basket in the middle of the living-room floor and then he threw the lasts, one after the other, into the old black Jøtul stove with its lion feet, and they burned well with an intense red flame.

'That's it, Arvid,' Dad said with an ugly laugh

and his face looked just like a rock. 'Now I'm a man without shoes!'

'I know,' Arvid said. 'Now you're a man with toothbrushes!'

And even though he was only one metre fifteen tall and pretty slight, his voice was so heavy with scorn that at first his dad stared at him and then went into the kitchen, and he slammed the door after him.

Ashes in His Mouth

The floor is cold to his bare feet. He can feel the cracks between the boards, and he tries to avoid even touching the floor. He takes his bearings from the dim light he knows must come from the half-open toilet door. Once there, he pulls down his underpants and pees, he's asleep, he dreams of a red bike racing across the shiny tarmac in Veitvetsvingen and the world around him explodes into green and blue and yellow. Then he walks back to his room like a little ghost in white pants, and his mother, who is watching him, does not know if she should wake him, or if she should laugh or cry. She does neither and, resigned, she fetches a wet cloth from the bathroom and wipes the floor for the fourth time this week, thinking it was a bad idea to leave the lamp on in the hall at night. The varnish cannot take much more.

Arvid is sleeping. Arvid is dreaming. He dreams he is falling through endless pipes, pipes that get darker and darker and resound with hollow echoes when he shouts all he can, but the echo fades and dies, and when he wakes he is screaming stifled screams into his duvet.

He dreams about animals with sharp teeth and long tails holding his body in a fierce grip, and when he wakes the duvet is wrapped tightly round his chest and he is staring into the dark with wide-open eyes. And then the duvet comes alive in his hands as he tries to untangle it from his body, and it coils and twists and he shouts:

'Mum! Dad! There are snakes in my bed!'

'No – there are – not.' His mother's drowsy voice hauls itself up from sleep in the next room.

'But there *are*!'

'Well, come in here then.'

Cautiously he draws his hands to his chest. He barely moves them. It must be done that way so the snakes don't notice, or else they might get angry and bite him. They have done it before.

A few minutes later he is on the floor. Ahead of him is the pool of light, the open door with its freedom from the darkness. Then there is a sound and he freezes, the grinding of sharp teeth and a rhythmic rustling sound. It is the tail, he can see it, swinging across the rug and it's rustling, rustling. He can see its eyes too, like two balls of fire burning his face.

'Mum! Dad! You've got to help me. There's a crocodile on the floor. I can't get past!'

'Nonsense. Come on now!'

'I can't! It will eat me up!'

A bed is creaking and then he hears the heavy footsteps across the floor. For a moment Dad fills the doorway and the world goes black. Arvid screams, everything whirls around him, he is dizzy, and he sinks to the floor, and then his dad enters, steps right through the crocodile and it's gone at once, and Dad grabs Arvid underneath the arms and lifts him up. Arvid falls asleep at once. Dad carries the limp body into the next room and shakes his head at the woman sitting up in the double bed like a question mark.

The following day his body is sluggish, his neck stiff, and it hurts when he moves his head.

He dreams he is flying high up, with a strong wind under his arms. It is wonderful, in his stomach there is a quiver. But when he wants to go down, he cannot, he is too light and then he rises and rises until he is all giddy and sick, and when he wakes he has a stomach virus and has to eat Marie biscuits and drink boiled water for several days.

He dreams that his dad's blue T-shirt with all the muscles inside it is suddenly empty and flabby and hanging there on a nail in a large empty attic room.

He dreams the house is full of ashes, there are ashes in his mouth and ashes in his pockets, and when he looks at himself in the mirror he has black lines all over his face from his fingers.

When he wakes, it is morning, but he doesn't feel like getting up even though it is Sunday.

The door opens and Mum enters the room.

14

'Hi, Arvid. You have to get up now. It's ten o'clock and we're going for a hike, remember?'

He turns to the wall.

'But Arvid, aren't you feeling well?'

He tries to see if he is ill, but he is not, he just doesn't want to get up. He wants to lie there gazing at the wall. There are two holes in the soft wall that his fingers have dug out when he's been in bed unable to sleep. He looks at the holes and thinks, there are two holes in the wall. I made them.

Mum goes to the window and pulls the curtains open. Light floods the room, for it is ten o'clock and summer.

'No!' he yells. Mum closes them and then she goes down the stairs.

'Frank!' she calls.

There are two holes in the wall. I made them, Arvid thinks. He raises a hand and runs his fingers around the edges, but he doesn't have the will to dig. He puts his hands under the pillow.

Dad comes in, the floorboards creak beneath his weight and he sits down on the edge of the bed and touches Arvid's shoulder.

'Hi there, chief, turn round so I can see you.'
Arvid turns stiffly, his hands covering his face.
Dad lifts him off the bed and holds him tight
to his body as he carries him out of the room.
Arvid can feel the solid muscles and the cloth
of the blue T-shirt.

In the bathroom Dad puts Arvid down on
the toilet seat and wraps a large towel around
his shoulders. Then he undresses and turns on
the shower. When the water is warm enough
he lifts Arvid, takes off his underpants and carries him into the shower, holding him close to
his chest while Arvid curls up and covers his
face. The hot water cascades over their heads
and Dad holds Arvid with one hand, wash-
ing him with the other, his face, chest, back,
between his legs, feet. Arvid starts crying. It
doesn't show because of the falling water, but
his dad notices a faint trembling. Then he turns
off the shower and places Arvid on a stool in
front of the basin, dries him gently and takes
his hands away from his face. Arvid looks in
the mirror and sees a very clean boy's face with

wet hair and it is his. Dad dries himself and puts on the blue T-shirt, tousles Arvid's hair and Arvid smiles.

'Come on, let's eat,' Dad says, and all of a sudden there is the wonderful strong aroma of fried bacon.

The Black Car

The day Arvid's granddad died was a Sunday, and most of the family had gone out to the cabin at the end of the Bunne Fjord. It was a red log cabin at the top of a slope that started gently by the road but then plunged down to the rocks on the shore. If you went up the stone steps and the door was not locked, you came into a narrow hall with three large windows looking out over the fjord. And then there was a sitting room and kitchen in one, but no one ever sat there because it was so dark. Upstairs was only one room with the beds down both sides, or in fact under the angle of the sloping roof, for its ends almost reached the floor. The floor was cold, there was a draught up between the boards, and the whole place reeked of damp wool carpets. If you didn't walk right in the middle of the floor, you were sure to bang your head and that was precisely what the grown-ups often did, especially at night when they went downstairs and outside for a pee. Even Granddad, who among many things was a Sunday-school teacher, swore blue murder when he hit his forehead on the beams.

Uncle Rolf solved this problem by going to the little window at the gable end, the one that wasn't above the front door, and he peed from there. This was not popular. Right beneath the window was Gran's rose bed and, although she had been dead for some years, Dad felt her memory should be treasured, and for him this rose bed had taken on such significance.

One time when Dad had been out doing what he did at night, he had seen what certain persons were up to and he roared so loud everyone jumped up in their beds:

'So you're standing there pissing on your mother's grave!'

Even though Arvid knew she was buried in the Eastern Cemetery.

Sitting by one of the large windows in the hall, Arvid could see the fjord twinkling like a vast piece of silver foil in a thousand small glints between the many spruce trees, far too many, Uncle Rolf said, half of them should be cut down so you could see what was happening on the water.

But that was how Arvid liked it, the spruce trees were like a strainer that only let the good light through so he couldn't see the ridge on the other side, for it was so sinister he dreamed about it at night. Dad felt the same way, or at any rate whenever Uncle Rolf piped up he said:

'Leave the spruces alone! If you want to study the boats you can go down to the jetty!' But Uncle Rolf didn't want to do that, if he could avoid it, for he was pretty fat, and when he had climbed up the steep path and all the steps that connected the cabin to the jetty his face was the same colour as the cabin, or even darker.

As far as the cabin was concerned, what Dad said usually went. Although they owned it together, it was Dad who had built it almost single-handedly. He had dragged the logs from the road, he had hammered and sawn and carried tons of sand and water enough for a medium-sized lake to mould the concrete steps and landings so the family wouldn't tumble into the fjord. That was why he was so strong and that was why the others were a little cowed when he was in a temper.

But Arvid wasn't cowed and Dad was not in a temper that often, and the only person who had done anything of any importance apart from Dad was Granddad, and he was going to die this Sunday, he was probably dead already, but they didn't know that yet.

Dad had a strong back. He was always doing stuff, as often as not with his back to Arvid, and it lived its own life inside the blue T-shirt with its large patches of dark sweat in the sun and the heat. Arvid could watch it for ages and feel at ease. Right now Dad was putting up the new flagpole, he had almost finished, and he had been into the forest himself to take down the tree he wanted.

'Pure theft,' Dad said, and that was the truth, for he had done it by night and dragged the trimmed tree back home before sunrise, and the T-shirt bulged and rippled as he tightened the lowest screws and Mum supported the pole. Uncle Rolf sat talking in a deckchair nearby.

'Not bad,' he said. 'A bit tall maybe, but I guess it'll be all right.' It was a long time since Dad had taken any notice of Uncle Rolf's opinion. He knew how he wanted it, and that was the way he did it.

'What do you think, Arvid?' he said. Arvid was sitting on the stone steps with his elbows on his knees, chin in his hands, and he said:

'It's fine, Dad. Tall and fine!'

'That's good,' Dad said, and then went to fetch the flag, and Mum snapped a picture with the old box camera held against her stomach.

A large print was hung on the wall at home above the bookcase. In the bottom left-hand corner Uncle Rolf had one arm in the air as if he were in charge.

The black car was not in the picture, and it could not have been, for it didn't arrive until later, but Arvid often glanced to make sure it really wasn't. In his memory, Dad standing by the flagpole and the black car had merged and he could not imagine one without the other.

He remembered the car as a Model T Ford and he knew well what a Model T looked like because they had a book with pictures at home, but it could not have been unless there was a veteran car rally that day, and there wasn't.

Big sister Gry was pretty. She had long blonde hair that matched her name, which meant daybreak, she was in the third class at school and could read Donald Duck comics much slower than Arvid.

'You can have them all when you've learned to read,' she had said, and Arvid often peered into the closet, where they were stacked in piles, calling to him with their speech bubbles, for that was where the secret was, but for now he let them drift past as clouds and covered his ears when Gry read aloud.

Gry waded along the shore with the water up to her knees, her blue dress tucked between her thighs, and Arvid could see her blonde hair bob up then disappear between the trees. Sometimes her head wasn't even there and all he could see was a bundle of blue clothes. Then she was bending down to pick up a mussel. When she had enough she laid them next to each other on a flat rock to dry. Later she cleaned them, made a hole at each end, threading them onto a piece of string, and she hung them around her neck like a chain. She looked nice, like a Red Indian girl.

Arvid stood up from the step, walked down the path and he felt the pine needles on his bare soles. It hurt in a way he liked. Behind him he could hear Uncle Rolf.

'Kari doesn't know what she's doing. Marrying a farmer! Christ!'

Uncle Rolf couldn't stand farmers, they had mud under their boots and said 'taters' instead of 'potatoes'. Uncle Rolf thought this was ridiculous.

'Alf's a great guy,' Arvid heard his dad say. 'Anyway, it's useful having a farmer in the family.' And their voices faded as Arvid clambered down the path.

Halfway down, on a ledge, Granddad's canoe lay keel-up on two stands. It was old, but still good enough and it had a nice tarry smell. It was about the only thing Granddad did at the moment, clean and fix the canoe, but he couldn't use it himself, he was too stiff and old to get into it. Dad said Arvid should come with him out on the water this summer, but Granddad said no.

'I don't want any kids in the canoe,' he said, 'it capsizes too easily, and I know kids can never sit still!' Dad might have been the strongest, but Granddad was the oldest, and since he had in fact done his share of work on the cabin, he could say no. Besides, the canoe was his. He said that very often.

Arvid met Aunt Kari, who had been out swimming. She had a bathing suit on and a towel wrapped around her shoulders. Aunt Kari had the softest lap in the world, even though she was not fat, and he could just close his eyes and remember what it was like to sit on. It was like sinking, like floating, whichever way he turned it was soft, and she smelt good. But he never got to sit there any more, not because he didn't want to, but because she thought he had grown too big.

Aunt Kari had curly black hair, she had the sun in her face and her body shone, and she said:

'You can't go down to the water on your own, Arvid!'

'Gry's there, and I can swim.'

'That's true, you can. You always knew how to swim.'

That was a fact. He had always been able to and didn't know what it was like when you couldn't. Many people thought that was odd.

But he never made it to the water that day. Before he got down to where Gry was he heard his mother's voice cut through the trees:

'Gry! Arvid! Come up here this minute!'

There was a sharp edge to her call, which meant they didn't dawdle as much as they usually would. Gry waded quickly to the shore, took Arvid's hand and together they hurried up the long steep hill. When they came to the top they were out of breath and there was a big black car in the little drive in front of the cabin. The engine was running and the car was humming and shaking, and the sun sparkled on the black paint. The man with the beret leaning on the car door they had seen before. It was Granddad's neighbour from Vålerenga.

Dad came bursting out of the cabin door. He had taken off his blue T-shirt and now he was pulling his white shirt on, his head was not through the neck yet and the two sleeves were flapping wildly in the air, and then he tripped and fell off the bottom step, and there was a stain on his shirt and he was furiously trying to wipe it off with his hand. Aunt Kari stood stock still in her bathing suit, the towel drooped onto the ground, and there were pine needles all over it. Uncle Rolf had actually got up from the deckchair and was on his way to the car.

Arvid turned away, for there was something so strange about his dad's face that he couldn't look. He looked at the treetops, he looked at the cabin roof, at the sky and the shimmering fjord. When he turned back, his dad was inside the car, and it reversed slowly towards the gate, pulled onto the road and stopped for a moment, and set off again and was gone. No one waved.

Aunt Kari went into the cabin to change, and her back was so naked she could have taken off her bathing suit and Arvid wouldn't have seen the difference.

'You two come here,' Mum said, and they too went in and she sat them at the table in the hall, and she looked at them, they looked at each other, and then she said:

'Be good children now, because your Grand-dad has died.'

And then they had cocoa and mocha biscuits, although it wasn't Saturday or anything, and as Arvid was blowing into his hot cup he was thinking:

Now it's Dad who's the boss around here, and I can go out in the canoe.

The King Is Dead

Beyond the house and the flagstone path was a large green lawn, and that was where he was sitting with his red fire engine. When he squatted like this, as he did on this particular day, all he could see was the lawn, and the whole world was nothing but green grass and a red fire engine. It was difficult to make it move because the grass was wet and quite long, he pushed and pushed, and then Gry came down the road and shouted:

'Hey, Arvid, guess what!'

He turned and the world became roads and houses, telephone wires and sky, a sky so big his head filled with air. He blinked.

No, he couldn't guess what.

'The king is dead. He slipped in the bathtub and died.'

Arvid put her words into his mouth. The king slipped in the bathtub and died. It didn't taste of anything. It didn't say a thing to him. He didn't know the king, although he did know there was a man called the king, but he had never seen the king and no one had a bathtub in their house. Just showers, there wasn't room for anything else, so he shrugged, turned to the fire engine, and Gry was disappointed and said:

'Hell, you're so little you don't understand one bit! Anyway, you've got to go in now. We're leaving soon.'

And when he looked up he saw his mother in the window. That was it, they had to go, he had forgotten. That was why he had his new trousers on. He stood up and then he saw it, close by. It was a bullfinch, that was for sure. Arvid had seen bullfinches many times, in the bullfinch tree and in the bird book he kept in his room. There was a picture of it and the letters underneath spelt 'bullfinch' when they were read out.

He knelt down, his trousers were wet at once

and stained with soil and grass, but he didn't notice and he held the bullfinch in his hand. It was so small, it was soft and warm. He could feel its heart beating against his fingers and he thought: Birds have a heart that beats!

He placed it on its thin legs. He let go and it toppled over and lay just as it had when he found it. The beak opened and closed, but it didn't say anything. Birds couldn't talk, but it moved its beak as if it wanted to.

He tried once more, but it fell again. His mind went blank. He couldn't leave, couldn't pretend he hadn't seen, but staying there didn't help either, for the bullfinch couldn't stand. He picked it up and threw it high in the air to see if it would fly, but it plummeted to the ground. He stood watching, it was red against the green grass, and then he started to cry. He couldn't leave, he would have to stay there, maybe for a long time.

Dad opened the window above and looked out.

'Arvid! What's up with you? Aren't you coming in?'

Arvid couldn't answer, he just pointed. Dad closed the window and after a little while he came out. Arvid stood where he stood. Dad bent down, picked up the bullfinch and said:

'Move away now, turn round and close your eyes.'

Arvid took a few steps, half-turned, but did not close his eyes. From the corner of one eye he saw his dad raise his arm and hurl the bird against the wall.

When he came in he was scolded for the stains on his trousers. But it was too late to change, and anyway he had only one pair of decent trousers, so he would have to go as he was, like a mucky pup.

Then the taxi arrived. It came rolling down the slope from the telephone box, parked by the dustbin, and all the kids in the street came to watch and asked if they were going on holiday.

'Kiss my arse,' Arvid said, and Mum said:

'Arvid, please! We're going to a funeral!' And then they got into the taxi and drove off.

Through the rear window he could see them standing on the tarmac.

At the funeral there were many grown-ups in black clothes, and first they had to enter an old yellow timber house called EBENEZER, Gry read the word aloud for Arvid. Inside EBENEZER Uncle Rolf was sitting in a chair looking sad. When the people in black came in they went over to him and said something in low voices and Uncle Rolf smiled a little and said thank you.

Uncle Rolf had once had a monkey, a big toy monkey with great shiny eyes hanging from a standard lamp. It used to hang from that lamp and look down at Arvid with a canny look on its face, and Arvid liked it so much that once when he and his mother were there to visit he asked:

'Can I have it?' He meant borrow, but that wasn't what he said.

'Christ, if the boy's envious he might as well have it as far as I'm concerned,' Uncle Rolf said with a smile that made Arvid wince.

At home Arvid took the monkey up to his

room to play with it, but it was different now, its eyes were dull and stupid so he tossed it in the bin under the sink. There Mum found it and she called to Arvid and asked what the hell the monkey was doing in the dustbin.

'It died,' Arvid said.

Now Granddad too was dead and Uncle Rolf had to live alone in the flat at Vålerenga, and he didn't like that because he was forty years old and had never been alone. Before, the whole family had lived in that flat with Granddad and Uncle Rolf, but it made Mum so worn down the doctor said she had to move as soon as possible and prescribed a new flat in a terraced house in Veitvet. At least that was what the woman next door said, and she ought to know because she often dropped by and spoke to Mum and drank coffee in the morning, and Arvid was sitting under the kitchen table playing, and he could hear them talking.

Arvid moved among the black stockings and the trousers, eating chocolate cake and listening. Above him voices buzzed and some were talking about the king, who had been such a steadfast Norwegian during the war although he was a Dane, and some talked about Granddad, who had been so very kind. Arvid didn't agree, even though it was true to say that Granddad gave him a chocolate bar each time he came to visit. But the chocolate tasted stale and it was because Granddad always bought enough chocolate for six months at a time and kept it all in the top drawer of the old dresser he had in the hall. That was the sensible thing to do, Dad said, but Arvid didn't think sensible was the same as kind. Once, Mum had said that Granddad treated her like a maid when they lived in Vålerenga, and when Dad defended him Mum lost her temper and said, and this I have to hear from a socialist!

A man came into EBENEZER, with his eyes downcast, not looking at anyone, but still he found Uncle Rolf and whispered something in his ear. Uncle Rolf got to his feet and made a gesture and then everyone stood up and they were on their way to the cemetery.

At the cemetery there was a chapel and they all went inside and sat down and they saw the priest on his knees mumbling in front of the altar. Then suddenly he got up, made the sign of the cross and turned to the assembly, his cassock swirling round his legs like a ball gown, and everyone could see his green-checked socks. Arvid laughed, but a glare from Uncle Rolf made him shut up. The priest's voice soared around the room and rose to the ceiling, and Arvid leaned back in the pew and looked up, but he couldn't make out what the priest was saying, and he fell asleep and didn't wake up until everyone was on their feet and ready to follow the coffin to the grave.

Outside it was pouring down, and Aunt Kari had to take one handle of the coffin even though she was a woman, for Uncle Rolf had been so upset after the service that he wasn't up to being a pall-bearer, and then the rain took a turn for the worse. Almost everyone in the small procession produced an umbrella, and those who didn't have one held newspapers over their heads, but the ones who carried the coffin couldn't cover themselves and the water was running from their hair, down their faces and dripping from their ears and noses. Arvid walked beside his dad and held on to his coat, the water splashing round his shoes, and you couldn't see the stains on them for everything was equally wet. Looking up, he saw his dad's face was soaking, and it now seemed so sad that Arvid felt he was going to cry, but he didn't want to because he didn't like Granddad and his plan was to hold back, but then he cried a little after all.

He closed his eyes as he walked and imagined his dad lying in the coffin, and Mum and Gry and he carrying it and after thinking about it for a while he felt his chest tightening. He could hear himself sobbing and making little howls, and one of the ladies in the procession came over and stroked his hair and said:

'Poor little boy, and you loved your grandfather so much. You shouldn't have been here at all.'

'No,' Arvid said, and meant the part about loving his Granddad, but the woman didn't get it and she scowled at Mum, and Mum blushed, rolled her eyes and sent Arvid a look as if he were Judas from the Bible. Arvid tightened his grip on Dad's coat.

They reached the hole in the ground where the coffin was to be lowered, and everywhere it was muddy and slippery, and water was trickling over the edges and into the grave and mud flowing from the nearby mounds of earth. The six pall-bearers walked cautiously over the last stretch and slowly set the coffin on two bars laid across the grave. As it was almost in place Dad slipped and fell onto one knee, the coffin tipped and banged down onto one bar, and Arvid gave a start and he heard Mum gasp behind him. Dad stood up again with a dazed smile and Arvid could see the huge muddy stain on his knee.

The priest came and started to speak, but Arvid could not hear what he was saying because of the rain and the wind blowing straight into his face, and the priest was gazing at Strømsveien and the cars droning past instead of looking at the coffin as he should have done, and his voice was lost. He dug out some slimy mud with his little spade and tried to toss it onto the coffin, but his eyes were elsewhere, so it missed and hit the edge of the grave and started a small landslide. Arvid shivered when he heard the mud splash at the bottom.

There were six ropes on the ground which the bearers were supposed to use to lower the coffin, and they each grabbed one and threaded it through a handle so they could hold both ends of their rope, but Dad didn't do what the others did. He tied it to the handle, and that was a mistake, Arvid could easily see that, everyone could, but no one said a word, just stared into the rain, pretending they hadn't noticed. When the coffin was on its way down, Dad's rope was too short and the further it was lowered the more Dad had to bend until he was balancing on the very brink.

'Dad! Let go!' Arvid yelled, and Dad let go and his rope went down with the coffin while the others got back theirs and placed them in a tidy heap.

Arvid could hear some strange noises behind him, and when he turned he saw Mum holding her hand in front of her mouth, her shoulders shaking and tears in her eyes, but behind her hand she was laughing, giggling even, and Arvid felt a trembling in his chest: what if Dad had not let go! He would have been down in the grave with Granddad, but Granddad was dead, the king was dead, the bullfinch was dead, but it didn't matter because Dad was alive and Arvid was alive and he started to jump up and down, he was smiling all over his face, and he ran over to his dad and buried his face in his wet coat. Dad stumbled a bit, but then he lifted Arvid up high and carried him back, and Arvid was almost certain that the sound from his dad's chest was laughter.

Like a Tiger in a Cage

When Arvid was outside playing, he would sometimes sit down in silence and think about his mother. Then he would try to draw her with a stick in the sand the way he was used to seeing her, in front of the kitchen counter with one of her striped aprons on. She would lean against the sink with the one hand, holding a cigarette with the other, and when without thinking she would run her hand through her hair there would be a hiss and then the smell of burning. Arvid often sat waiting for that.

She'd looked the way she always had for as far back as he could remember, and she still did right up until the day he happened to see a photograph of her from before he was born, and the difference floored him. He tried to work out what could have happened to her, and then he realised it was time that had happened and it

43

was happening to him too, every second of the day. He held his hands to his face as if to keep his skin in place and for many nights he lay clutching his body, feeling time sweeping through it like little explosions. The palms of his hands were quivering and he tried to resist time and hold it back. But nothing helped, and with every pop he felt himself getting older.

He cried, and said to his mother:

'I don't want to get older. I want to stay like I am now! Six and a half, that's enough, isn't it?' But she smiled sadly and said, to every age its charm. And time withdrew to the large clock on the wall in the living room and went round alone in there, like a tiger in a cage, he thought, just waiting, and Mum became Mum again, almost like before.

She used to work at the Freia chocolate factory, and those were the good days, for no one could deny that chocolate found its way from Grünerløkka to where they lived in Veitvet. But all good things must come to an end, and now she had a cleaning job at the music school in the evenings and that was not the same. One time when Arvid was allowed to come with her even though it was late, he looked for things they could take home, but sheet music was no good, and the pianos were too heavy.

Now Dad was the one to sing Arvid to sleep in the evening, and that was not the same at all. Every night he sang the one about the cat stuck in the spruce tree or something. Arvid never understood what it was really about, and anyway he couldn't care less. He soon realised that the only way he could escape the song was to fall asleep as quickly as possible, and Dad boasted and said it was his talent as a singer that made him succeed. There was only one song that was worse, and that was 'When the Fjords Turn Blue', but that one Dad only sang when there were guests and they'd had a drink or two. Then Mum went into the kitchen and waited there until he had finished.

Sometimes, when his yodelling was at its worst, Dad went out onto the balcony because he wanted a view of the land as he sang. 'When the fjords turn blue!' he roared, but except for the bullfinch tree there was nothing out there, only the terraced houses and the tenement buildings, and then Mum would drag Dad back into the living room and say:

'Now you damn well pull yourself together, Frank!'

And he did, at least when he'd had no more than two of those drinks.

But there were other things, Arvid could tell, for he didn't always go to sleep at once, he just pretended to so his dad would stop singing. There were voices seeping up from the kitchen. They slipped out through the crack under the kitchen door, glided along the rug in the hall, over the worn carpet in the living room and up the stairs, wearing themselves shiny and sharp on the way. Sitting at the top of the stairs, Arvid could feel the voices skid off his body. He was cold, but inside him there was a heat, like a little flame only he could put out, and one day he would do that, he thought, put it out when they least expected and turn to ice, but he would never let anyone else make the flame go out, not even let them come near.

The voices grew louder, the kitchen door

must have been open now, and he heard a bang and the sound of something breaking. He knew what it was, it was the last plate in the set they had brought with them from their life in Vålerenga, and it was a sound Arvid knew well because it was he who had broken the last but one. It happened one day when he tried to carry a knife, a fork, a glass and a plate to the kitchen counter all in one go. The plate slithered out of his hands and smashed into a thousand pieces on the kitchen floor, and it startled Arvid and he was afraid his dad would get mad since he was so fond of that set, or so he said, but only Mum saw what happened and she said:

'Don't worry about it, Arvid. I couldn't care less.' And she looked like she didn't as she swept up the pieces and threw them in the bin.

Now Arvid could hear someone clattering around in the hall, and then Mum came rushing into the living room, boots on, wearing her raincoat and gloves, trying furiously to tie her headscarf under her chin.

With one angry movement she snatched the pack of Cooly cigarettes from the coffee table, turned round and saw Arvid sitting on the second step from the top.

'So that's where you are, Arvid?' she said in a strange voice.

'Yes.'

'Aren't you cold?'

'I am.' He huddled up and was truly cold now.

'You go upstairs to bed. I'll be back soon. I'm just going out for a little walk.'

He got up and his legs hurt, they had gone stiff, and as he was about to enter his bedroom he heard the front door slam.

In the next room his big sister, Gry, was sleeping. He went in and shook her by the shoulder.

'Gry! Wake up!'

Gry twisted away and buried her face in the pillow.

'What is it?' she mumbled from the depths.

'Mum is out walking again.'

Gry rolled out of bed and together they went

to the bedroom window. Outside it was night and wet, and they could see her striding out beneath the street lamp on her way up the slope, and there were raindrops glittering in the light above her headscarf. She was the only person out on the street, and when she was gone, past the shopping centre and towards Trondhjemsveien, it was deserted, only the street lamps and the rain.

They knew where she was going, even though they were never allowed to come with her, and anyway she walked so fast there would have been no point, but she had told them. She walked up Trondhjemsveien, on the left-hand side, as far and as fast as she could. When she reached Grorud or thereabouts, she crossed the road and came all the way back at the same insane tempo, smoking non-stop. Arvid had seen how the pack of Cooly dwindled.

'Why does she go out in weather like this?' Arvid said.

'She has to, don't you see?'

'How do you know?'

'We women know that sort of thing, Arvid,'

Gry said, laying her hand on Arvid's shoulder.

'Jesus,' Arvid said, wrenching himself away. 'You're only in the fourth grade.'

And then he went back to his room. He had decided to stay awake until Mum returned, but he fell asleep and when he woke up he had wet the bed. His mind made a half-hearted attempt to remain in the trough of sleep, but in the end it had to come up and he felt that all-too-familiar freezing-cold sensation around his hips.

He lay quite still and tried to go back to sleep, squeezing his eyes shut and thinking of sheep and clouds and all those things that Uncle Rolf had taught him to do, but it was rubbish and didn't help, and he had to get up. Carefully he took off his sodden underpants and put them under the dresser. This was his secret trick and it always worked. Every time he had wet himself he put the clammy underpants under the dresser and the next night they were gone. It was like magic, but he tried not to think about it. He didn't want the magic to go away.

Mum was back. He could hear her light steps

on the stairs and he jumped into clean under-pants and got back into bed, close to the wall, and he almost curled around the wet patch he could do nothing about, but he knew it would be gone by morning. Mum came in to see if he was under the duvet. He pinched his eyes shut to show he was asleep, but she came up close and said:

'Are you still awake, Arvid?'

'Mm.'

'You should have been asleep hours ago.'

'Mm. I know. But I have slept.' He wondered if he should open his eyes, and then he did, and she sat down on the edge of his bed and stroked his hair.

'Were you afraid for Mummy, Arvid?'

Afraid? He was not. She always went for these walks when there was something up, and even if he didn't like her going out when the weather was bad, he had never been afraid. He shook his head, but then he remembered something.

'Mum?'

'Yes?'

'Why do you cross the road? I mean, why do you cross the road when you're almost in Grorud and you're on your way back?'

'Because I don't want to walk with the cars heading in the same direction as me.'

'Why not?'

'Because it makes me feel they are all going away and I'm left standing there. You see?'

'Mm. But what do you do?'

'I don't do anything. I think.'

'About what?'

'Nothing you have to bother your little head about.'

She thought he didn't understand a thing. Everyone thought he was stupid because he was only three feet seven inches tall. But he was not stupid, and he knew well enough what went through her head when she was out there walking, and when she said, 'Goodnight,' turned off the light, and went downstairs he was absolutely sure, because then he could hear them down below.

'So you're back. You've let off some steam, have you?'

'Oh, that's so typical of you, Frank! You don't understand a thing! You just say wait and we have to think this over, but I don't want to wait, do you understand? I'm not twenty any more!'

Next morning when he woke he had slept longer than usual, the room was light and underneath him he had a clean sheet. How that could have happened he didn't know, it was more magic, and as soon as he realised he tried to think about something else.

Everywhere it was strangely quiet, he could not hear a sound, and he was the early riser, always awake before Gry, while Mum lay in bed reading, as she did no matter what time he poked his head round the door, and Dad would be in the kitchen making breakfast before he left for work. Then Arvid used to sneak down and stand by the kitchen counter eating a slice of bread, trembling with cold until Dad tousled his hair and left with the bag under his arm.

Now Dad was away, and when Arvid looked into Gry's room, her bed was empty. He tiptoed down the stairs to the living room, and that was empty too, but the cellar door was open, and if he listened carefully he could hear a faint splashing of water he knew came from the laundry room, and that meant his mother was down there.

He was all alone in the flat, and it gave him such a chilling sensation of freedom that for a moment he stood still, it was so unexpected. He could do whatever he wanted, and then he knew exactly what he wanted to do. He quickly fetched a chair and placed it by the bookcase, stepped up onto it, and started to climb. He knew it was all right, the shelving was screwed into the wall. When he swung himself up to the very top he almost knocked off the old vase they had brought with them from Vålerenga, and even though Mum might not have cared about that either he managed to catch it at the last moment.

Carefully he straightened up. It was a long way down to the floor, and for a fraction of a second he was balancing on the edge of the bookcase and felt the rush of fire in his stomach. Then he raised his arms as high as he was able to, which was not that high, but it was enough to touch the large clock. He pushed it off its hook, and for a moment it rested in his hands, and Jesus it was heavy, and then it tipped over and sailed through the air and landed on the floor with a crash that was a hundred times louder than he had expected.

He stood on top of the bookcase in his underpants, and they were slowly getting wet, and he looked down at the splinters of glass, the scattered cogwheels and the two clock hands wobbling round in a meaningless void. From the cellar he heard the click-clack of his mother's steps, 'Arvid! Arvid!' she cried, and then he pushed his face to the wall and held his hands to his ears.

Fatso

They called him Fatso, and fat he *was*, that is his belly was fat, it stuck out like an over-inflated balloon and was peculiar to look at from the side, but otherwise Fatso was slight. It was a long time since Fatso had used a belt for his trousers, because it just slipped under his belly, and then his trousers fell down and his wife was so embarrassed, she said, that she told him to find another solution. That's why he wore braces, or 'guy ropes' as Dad said on the sly, and that was how he looked, like a tent.

No one called him Fatso to his face. 'Bomann' they said, for that was his name, and as far as his belly was concerned there was only one thing wrong with it, Dad said, it was always full of beer. Builders drink a lot of beer, every-one knows that, and Arvid knew it too. But Fatso didn't just drink beer; he had the biggest and most sophisticated home-brew kit in the street.

There was bubbling and sputtering in almost every flat along the road, and those who didn't have a kit themselves shared with a neighbour. The smallest set-up was Thomassen's on the corner, but that was to be expected, Dad said, for Thomassen worked for the police and had to be discreet.

It wasn't long since Thomassen got his own kit, and until then especially Fatso, but not only him, had worried that Thomassen would report them, and great was the relief when the machinery was set up under his kitchen sink. Jon Sand, who lived next door to Thomassen and was the same age as Arvid, said all the neighbours had chipped in for the kit. They had been talking about it in the laundry room, and Thomassen couldn't refuse when he was given it for his birthday. But Jon was always making out he knew just about everything, and it was common knowledge that his mother and father were the biggest gossips in Veitvet, so Arvid didn't pay it any mind.

One day Arvid's mother called him the way she always did.

'Arvid! Dinner!' she yelled, and it was really annoying, why did she always have to shout so damn loud, she was the only person who did that, and the other kids grinned and said, 'Arvid, your Mum's shouting for you,' as if he hadn't heard! But it was Thursday and offal, and unlike the rest of the family Arvid thought offal was really good (animal fodder, said Dad, cheap, said Mum) so he set off at a run. He ran a lot, he couldn't keep his legs still for more than a couple of minutes at a time, and he raced like a terrier up the flagstone path in front of the house.

Fatso was sitting on the front steps reading *Arbeiderbladet*, and Arvid could have sworn he stuck his leg out although it would be hard to prove, but anyway he fell flat on his face and screamed an air-quivering God damn it. Fatso lowered his paper, lifted his index finger and said:

'You're not allowed to swear, you're too little!'

'Mind your own business, Fatso!' Arvid howled, for his knee hurt like the devil and tears gushed from his eyes when it started to bleed. But he had said what he wasn't supposed to say out loud, too loud, he knew it at once, and now it was too late to take it back.

Fatso stood up in one surprisingly quick movement considering the huge belly he was carrying.

'What did you say?!' he said, grabbing Arvid's shoulder.

'Fatso!' Arvid screamed, for now he was both frightened and defiant, and Fatso dragged him hobbling to the door where it said JANSEN, and just then Arvid's mother opened it.

'Did you hear what he said, *fru* Jansen?' said Fatso.

'No, Bomann,' Mum said. 'I've just got here, haven't I. So, what did he say?'

'He called me Fatso,' Fatso said. 'No one calls me Fatso!'

'No one does, Bomann.'

'No, they don't? This whelp of yours just did. Fatso, he said. No one calls me Fatso. I won't have it and I bet he didn't come up with it himself!'

'I don't understand, Bomann,' Mum said. 'I've never heard anyone call you anything except Bomann, that's for sure, and the boy is only eight years old. Why should that bother you?' Mum said, and Arvid, who was a bit annoyed with her because she was lying, was impressed too, for she lied so beautifully, she didn't even blush, just looked at Fatso with her brown eyes in such a good-natured way, and Arvid had never heard her say anything but Fatso when they were by themselves.

'I'll tell you something for nothing,' Fatso said, 'if I ever hear that whelp call me Fatso again I'll do him over!'

'Right, Bomann, I think you should go and sit on your step and finish reading that paper of yours instead of standing here playing the bogeyman,' Mum said as softly as she could, and then she dragged Arvid indoors for dinner and offal.

Now Arvid had an enemy for life. For a long time they walked around hating each other

from a distance, and whenever Arvid walked
past his front-door steps, Fatso shook his fist
and Arvid stared down at the flagstones and
hissed:

'Fatso, Fatso, Fatso Beerbelly!'

Every payday Fatso got drunk. It was not un-
usual, he got drunk on other days as well, but
on payday he was drunk before he got home,
and even though his wife didn't mind a drop
herself, she never took it well, for she was
afraid he would squander or completely blow
his money, and she could get pretty angry and
loud. Not that she stood on the front step rant-
ing and raving like certain others, outdoors she
was as mild and gentle as a lamb, but indoors it
was a different matter. It wasn't difficult to hear,
for Fatso lived next door to Arvid and his family, and Selvaag the contractor had taken quite
a few short cuts with insulation when the terraced houses were built. He'd taken short cuts
on most things, Dad said. The gaps between
the floorboards were so wide that the little
ones tripped in the cracks and were slower to

walk than other children, at least that's what Dad claimed, so Fatso didn't dare go home when he'd been drinking after work on pay-day. Instead he went up to the edge of the forest on the other side of Trondhjemsveien and lay down to sleep. Everyone knew this except his wife, for no one told her. Every single pay-day night the light burned in Fatso's kitchen, and there she sat waiting for him and didn't know where he was.

And it was summer and Saturday, and Arvid got up early as he always did when he had no school. On weekdays they had to drag him half-unconscious from his bed. It was strange and even he didn't know why it was like this. But on his days off he jumped on his bike at the crack of dawn and headed for the forest and pedalled along the paths, did motocross and was Basse Hveem. Uncle Rolf had given him a helmet and he had it on. Dad didn't like it much, do you have to put that bowler on your skull, he would say. He was embarrassed by all sorts of things, like when Arvid wore his Scout uniform outdoors. You look like a Christmas tree, Dad said, and anyway the Scouts are middle class, and it seemed as if he preferred Basse Hveem, who probably wasn't so middle class.

Arvid stormed down the last hill, swerved into the horse field in the true style, waved modestly to an invisible crowd and dismounted. This was where the horses from the Bjerke Trotting Stadium lazed around, priming themselves for Sunday, and all the kids had their own favourites. Arvid's was Thunder, who was brown with white socks and a white mane and was such a handsome sight when he raced around that you couldn't stop yourself from running.

Arvid sat down on a rock to rest and that was when he saw a man curled up under a bush. He jumped up and stared, for there was something familiar about that bundle, and he heard sounds that made the hairs on the back of his neck stand up. The bundle turned and looked at him, and it was Fatso. One brace strap had slipped off, and his shirt had ridden up and his belly spilled out, and it was horrible to see.

Fatso was crying, that was the sound Arvid had heard, and it was the worst thing he had ever experienced, for he had never seen a grown man cry. It was something you stopped doing around the time you were confirmed, the way you stopped wearing nappies a little earlier. At least he hadn't seen an adult wearing nappies. Those things were automatic, everyone knew that. In a few years he would have hairs round his willy and women got children when they married and so on. He knew about this stuff, you just had to take things as they came without whining, Dad said, and Arvid agreed.

'You're crying,' Arvid said.

'The hell I am,' Fatso said. 'It's been raining, right. And I've been lying here and haven't dried myself, but I will now.'

That was just nonsense because the forest was tinder-dry when Arvid set out and it had not rained for weeks, so Fatso was lying and knew that Arvid knew it and standing there was getting unpleasant.

'Would you do me a favour?' Fatso asked.

'Can't,' Arvid answered. 'You're my enemy.'

'Yes, I know, you're mine too, that's not the point. Haven't you heard of an armistice?'

Arvid hadn't, but he couldn't admit it, so he just said:

'What do you want me to do?'

'Could you take this wallet …?' Fatso twisted round and reached into his back pocket, his belly stuck out even more and Arvid looked away. 'Could you take this and cycle down and give it to my wife? It's not as full as it should have been, but it's not as empty as she thinks.' He held out the wallet to Arvid, but Arvid didn't feel like taking it.

'Come on, I'm not a leper!' Arvid didn't know what a leper was, but if it had anything to do with his belly or his crying, he was not so sure. He carefully took the wallet by the one corner.

'She must have it, see, otherwise she goes mad. Tell her I'm coming home, but not quite yet. And then come back and report. And, boy, you can help yourself to a krone.'

The wallet was like a brick, it just got heavier and heavier, and he had to hold it close to his chest with his left hand and steer with his right. That was not easy down the hills in Slettaløkka, but he managed. He didn't touch the money.

Once down by the terraced house he was so nervous he was shaking, but he rang Fatso's doorbell and his wife answered, and looked like she had just got up, but she had all her clothes on and there was a light on in the kitchen even though the sun was boiling. He gave her the wallet, said what he had been told to say, and she stood gaping at him as he pedalled down the pathway like a crazy man.

The hills on the way back up were as tough and unforgiving as blue clay, and several times he thought maybe he should turn round, but he didn't, and when he reached the top Fatso was sitting on a tree stump crying again. His shirt and braces were back in place, and when he heard the cycle wheels on the gravel he looked up and asked how it had gone.

'Fine,' Arvid said.

'Good,' Fatso replied, and there was a short silence, and then Fatso said,

'Arvid?'

Arvid started at the sound of his name, because Fatso never used his name, he always said 'you' or 'the whelp' or 'boy' or something along those lines, and Arvid wished he had never heard it.

'It's all right if you call me Fatso, Arvid,' Fatso said, 'it doesn't matter. You are the only person who had the guts to say it to my face even though I know everyone calls me Fatso behind my back. You just call me Fatso!'

Fatso forced a pale smile through the tears, but Arvid knew he would never call Fatso 'Fatso' again, and when he later tried to say 'Bomann' aloud to himself it felt as if he had a large cold marble in his mouth, and then he knew he would never talk to him again, ever.

People Are Not Animals

He held the piece of bread and jam as level as possible and at the same time tried to flip the little animal over the sand pile it was so desperately struggling to climb, but it kept falling back down. It was a beetle with yellow stripes down its black back, not pretty at all, almost ugly, but it was so sad when it tumbled backwards, so he thought he had to help.

And in the end he did it, an elegant twist of his foot and the beetle was over, and even if he didn't expect any gratitude, beetles are quiet creatures, then at least a sign, a wave from one of its legs perhaps, but no. The beetle just headed straight for the next sand heap probably thinking Arvid would give assistance once again, like some super-hero, Superman perhaps, but now this was it. Disgusting insect. With the tip of his shoe he kicked the beetle, and it flew in a large arc over the sandpit, but instead of crashing into the log on the other side it unfolded two small wings, looped the loop and banked beautifully across the road and was gone behind Johansen's Opel Kadett. Why the hell didn't it do that straight away?

Now it had gone there was nothing else to concentrate on, and he knew that soon he would have to turn round. He could hear them, their soles scraping sand on the tarmac, and they were whispering to each other.

He stared down at his feet as he took a bite of his bread, and they were odd, seen from above, large and alien, as though they didn't belong to his body at all. He had checked in the mirror a few times, but they were not the same feet at all, because the ones in the mirror were OK. Those strange feet sticking out, and the knees. But the knees were his, he could tell by the grazes. Yet they were strange, nobbly and big, and then someone laughed a nasty laugh, and he would rather have been beaten up than listen to what was coming now, but it came anyway and there was nothing he could do about it.

'Arvid fucks his mum! Arvid fucks his mum!'

They chanted in unison, but that didn't make it more true, he was only eight years old and hadn't fucked anyone, and so far he had flatly denied that anyone did such a thing and least of all his mother, but if there was one thing the boys knew about it was his opinions on fucking. That was why they went for him as soon as they had a chance.

'Arvid fucks his mum! Arvid fucks his mum!'

They would not stop, they just chanted louder and louder, and he felt his fury rising as it always did, even though he tried with all his might to hold it back, and perhaps the worst thing was the way he blushed. With willpower alone he tried to stop it from spreading, but he failed, for just to say that one word aloud was like pulling a trigger, and he had no control over anything, and then he turned and through a mist he saw their faces expanding into huge grins.

It was too late to stop now, so he just smacked

71

his sandwich into the face of the boy closest to him, splashing jam everywhere. The little group howled with joy and shouted:

'Here it comes! Here it comes! He's lost it now! Look at him!'

He flailed around, aiming for a face, hit one, maybe two, but then there was a thud above his right eye and he went down with a boy on top of him, and it was Bjørn, who else. Bjørn, who was ten years old and almost a teenager, who had seen all kinds of things and was as strong as the bear he was named after, and Bjørn grabbed Arvid's hair and forced his head back so they were staring into each other's eyes. Arvid could feel the tarmac rubbing against the back of his head, and then with rage in his voice Bjørn shouted:

'When will you get it, you moron. People fuck, or else there wouldn't be any babies!'

'Only pigs fuck!' Arvid screamed back.

'No! People fuck just like pigs or dogs or horses or monkeys in a cage! Get that into your thick skull!' Bjørn was almost in tears he was so angry.

'People aren't animals! People are people!'

'Jesus, you're so hopeless,' Bjørn said. 'You won't even get through school.' He got up, turned to the others standing round them in a circle, and said:

'We're wasting our time. He's a complete idiot. He'll end up in remedial class and become an arselicker.'

And so they left, shaking their heads, roaring with laughter, and Arvid was lying on the road, staring up into the air, and he was crying. But they were right, he knew that now, for he had asked Dad, and although Dad coughed and looked away and both of them blushed, he didn't deny it. It was the only explanation, but it was a lot to take for someone who had just stopped believing in God.

People fucked. Or else there wouldn't be any babies. That's the way it was. But he would never do it, wouldn't want to or dare to or manage to, and he couldn't care less whether he had children or not. But he felt strangely sad when he thought about that particular thing.

Call Me Ali Baba

He believed all the hollows in the fields by the women's prison were caused by bombing. He imagined that the world was once completely flat and the bombs that fell during THE WAR, in his mind like big heavy bumble bees, had formed the landscape the way it was now.

When Dad talked about THE WAR, and he often did, for he had been a part of it, Arvid could picture these hollows, and when they were playing in the little valley they called Dumpa it struck him that some of the bombs must have been really big.

When he found out that no bombs had fallen around where he lived, he couldn't believe it, for the image of the rolling fields and the bumble-bee bombs had become part of the boy he was, and there was nothing to put in their place.

He thought the women's prison was a church, and it looked like a church, but although he knew there were always people inside he never saw anyone coming out. It was so quiet in the courtyard behind the high wire fence, the gravel was red, like nowhere else in the district, and the tall doors were always locked. Sometimes there was a black car in the courtyard, but he had never seen it coming or going.

He knew there were always people inside for when he played in the fields he saw faces at the windows, and when the women inside waved he waved back, and when the wind was blowing from the right direction their voices fluttered like scraps of paper on the shining autumn air. But when they shouted to him, he ran, and after he was told it was not a church he only played there if he forgot he shouldn't.

One time when he did forget, there was a woman standing at a window shouting:

'Give my love to Joakim!' And she started to laugh aloud when she saw him run. He covered his ears, for he didn't want to hear, but it was too late and he realised he would always remember the name: Joakim.

A few days afterwards Dad read aloud from the newspaper about someone who had escaped from prison and Arvid knew at once who it must have been.

That night she came to him in his dreams and she shouted Joakim! Joakim! until he woke and sat up and he too called Joakim! Joakim! and Mum came bursting into his room and said, for God's sake, what is going on here?

Between the high rises and the terraced houses there was a barn. It was red with large grey peeling patches and had stood there for ever, for as long as he had lived, and even though Dad said it was part of a farm that had been there before, Arvid couldn't care less. The barn was there, and was the Barn.

'Let's go and play in the Barn,' the children said to one another, because it was a good place to play, and the fact that they were not allowed made it even better. The grown-ups said it was because the place was falling down, but Arvid thought why would a barn that had stood for as long as he had lived suddenly decide to collapse right now?

The Barn had a traditional ramp and a big barn door that was shut with a bolt and a big padlock. Arvid and Jon Sand had tried to open it many times, Jon had even tried with a firecracker he had swapped with his big brother for a copy of *Illustrated Classics*, and had stuffed it into the lock. There had been a bang, but that was it. The lock was still intact and the door still closed.

They jumped from the barn ramp, and the trick was to jump from as high as possible. The higher, the tougher. It could be dangerous, but until now two broken legs were the worst that had happened and that wasn't too bad.

Arvid was almost up by the door when he jumped, and there was such a wonderful rush in his belly when he leaped, and he rarely hurt himself because he was so light. The big boys called him Death Diver, and whenever they said that he smiled inside. But he didn't smile with his lips, he just curled his top lip the way his mother had shown him that Elvis did when he was at his peak, and if there was something Mum knew about it was Elvis. When they played Elvis on the radio she sat at the kitchen table with a cigarette and sang and smoked and knew all the songs by heart, and every morning she sang 'It's Now or Never' in the bathroom.

Arvid had practised in front of the mirror in the hall and after a while he was so good at curling his lip that many people thought he had been born like that.

But Jon was the one who could jump furthest. Arvid did the best he could and yet he was always half a metre behind.

'Your legs are too short,' Jon said. 'See for yourself, your knees are almost in your shoes!' But that couldn't be right because the doctor at school had said he had a well-balanced body, and when he asked his mother what that meant, she said every part of his body was in its right place and that was a good thing.

In any case Arvid thought it was better to be the Death Diver than an ordinary long jumper. Jon probably thought so too, Arvid guessed, but he didn't say that, because they were friends and shared whatever fame and glory came their way.

'I wonder what's inside,' Arvid said. They stood there with leaves in their hair, sand in their shoes, staring at the shabby old barn, their knees giving way and their legs shaking after a long but happy stint of jumping.

'Comics,' Jon said. 'Newspapers.'

'Comics?'

'Yes, *Donald Duck*, *Texas*, *Wild West*, *Prairie*, *Arbeiderbladet*, *Jukan*, *Morgenposten*. When they had a paper collection, they brought it all here to the Barn. My big brother said so, for he saw them.'

'*Texas* comics?'

'Yes, dammit.'

'But then we have to get inside before it's too late!'

'Sure, but how?'

They looked at the big walls and felt helpless, the solid barn door and the foundations, and then they both saw it at the same time. The Barn didn't have proper foundations like terraced houses, it was standing on a square of big boulders, and between the rocks there were gaps. How could they have missed them?

They ran round the Barn searching for the biggest gap and when they found it Jon almost threw himself in, he squirmed and kicked and shoved until he was stuck, and Arvid had to pull him out again.

'It's no good,' Jon said, holding his hand to a graze on his cheek. 'You try.'

Arvid peered into the black hole, and now he wasn't so keen. Suppose there were some-one inside, you couldn't know that before-hand, suppose *she* was in there hiding while everyone was searching, and once he thought about her he could almost hear her and he was sure that was how it was: she was inside, in the dark, waiting for him.

But Jon was standing there, looking excited, and he had done his bit, he even had grazes on his cheek, and it was suddenly impossible for Arvid to say he didn't dare.

He felt a chill inside as he stuck his head in and began to push himself between the rickety stones. It was so dark inside he didn't know whether his eyes were open or shut, and after deciding he wouldn't go any further he felt Jon grab his feet and push him all the way in. It was a tight squeeze, the sharp stones scraped against his stomach and one of his jacket buttons came off, and then he was on the ground inside and screamed:

'Shit, what did you do that for?' But then he shut up because it was so low under the floorboards above him that his voice bounced back and boomed in his ears and filled up the dark.

'Because you're so damned slow,' Jon said from outside. 'Do we want the comics or not?'

Arvid groped with his hands like a blind man at the movies, afraid of touching something strange or perhaps *someone* strange, and wasn't that breathing he could hear? At any rate something was moving, there was a rustling of paper, and then he felt something brush against his thigh, something soft and living. He gasped for air, the hairs on his neck stood up, he went stiff and straightened up, but instead of hitting his head on the floor above he was suddenly able to stand upright. And then he realised he had his eyes closed, and when he opened them, it was no longer dark.

There was a hole in the floor. He had his head and shoulders up inside the Barn and streams of light came flowing between the wide cladding boards and, when he looked around him, he saw an ocean of newspapers and comics.

He seized the nearest bundle, tore at the string, and it snapped with a twang, and an avalanche of magazines came crashing towards him, sending swirls of dust up into the air. Arvid grabbed as many as he could hold, shrank back down through the floor and crawled fast towards the aperture of light, where Jon was standing unharmed outside, no ice in his stomach and only a graze to his cheek.

'Wow!' said Jon as magazines, newspapers and comics suddenly came flying from the crack in the wall, followed by Arvid with a look in his eyes that Jon had never seen in his friend before.

They sifted through them and it turned out

that, apart from three copies of *Alle Kvinner*,
four of *Aftenposten* and six of *Reader's Digest*,
there were two of *Tarzan* and five of *Texas* they
had never ever seen. Arvid fingered the spot
on his jacket where the button used to be and
said:

'Call me Ali Baba!' And then he laughed.

Jon wasn't the sort of boy to keep secrets,
and soon the story about Arvid's exploits was
doing the rounds. At the same time the grown-
ups had started to talk about the Barn being
demolished, and about time too, Dad said, that
dump is a danger to life and limb, you keep
away from it, Arvid! I will, said Arvid, but out
in the streets panic ran like a terrified squir-
rel between the houses, children exchanged
looks and thought, so close to the riches and
maybe their newly discovered way into the
Barn would be lost and gone for ever!

One evening Jon knocked on the door to ask
if Arvid could come out. His big brother wanted
to talk to him, Jon said, and Arvid asked his
dad if he could. Dad glanced at his watch and
said:

84

'Have you done your homework?' even though he knew full well that he had, Arvid always did it the minute he came home from school.

'Yes, I have,' he said.

'OK, half an hour,' Dad said as he always did. Arvid could have asked at ten o'clock on a Sunday night and his dad would have replied, 'OK, half an hour.'

Outside it was dark and wet, and although it was not raining, you felt the damp air settle on your skin at once and it was good to breathe. Arvid liked it when it was dark and wet, he felt tucked up in a woollen blanket and hidden away, yet able to walk wherever he wished.

Trond Sand was fifteen years old and waiting by Thomassen's with a cigarette in his mouth that he smoked, and Arvid could see the glow bobbing up and down like the lanterns at sea when they took the ferry to visit Gran and Granddad in Denmark.

'Hi, Death Diver,' Trond said.

'Hi,' Arvid said with a slight curl of the lip.

'I heard you got into the Barn. You're the

only one who made it. Pretty neat, if you ask me.'

'Ah, it was nothing special.'

'It was, trust me,' Trond said, taking a drag from the cigarette, blowing smoke out again and it looked white and ghost-like against the black sky. Trond flicked the butt and it twirled round and landed with a hiss on the shiny, wet tarmac.

'You know Bandini?' he said.

Stupid question, Arvid thought, everyone knows Bandini. Bandini was the strangest man in Veitvet, and that was saying a lot, for in Veitvet there was no shortage of strange men. Bandini was Italian and an artist, the only one Arvid had ever seen close up. He had a walking stick and wore a green army jacket and his long hair was tied in a knot on top of his head. Mum thought that was charming. Bandini was also the politest man she knew, and in this block everyone and his brother could learn a little from that, she said, casting a meaningful glance at Dad, who might as well have his Sunday-school fees back, for it had been a complete waste of money.

On the lawn outside his house Bandini had placed a car engine painted blue, and when there were enough people in the street he would go out and pat the engine and say, this, my friends, is great art. But Dad said it was a Ford Anglia engine, and it was not great art at all, it was a load of crap. He said that because he once had an Anglia himself, but when he started working at Jordan he couldn't afford a new car after the Anglia packed up.

Most of the time Bandini sat in his flat painting naked ladies. At the kiosk he was Knoff's biggest customer for *Cocktail*, for it was not easy to get live models in Norway, Dad said, who liked Bandini well enough, for he had also been to THE WAR, in Italy, but had fled because a man called Mussolini wanted to cut off his head.

'Of course I know Bandini,' Arvid said.

'He's moving back to Italy,' Trond said. 'He can't manage the hills up to Trondhjemsveien any longer, and Mussolini croaked fifteen years ago, so there's no problem going back.'

Trond lit another cigarette and went on:

'So he gave all his magazines to the paper collection, and I was thinking you might do me a favour. Get my drift?'

'No,' Arvid said.

'You don't wanna do me a favour?'

'Yes, I do. I mean what favour?'

Trond rolled his eyes. 'Bandini's mags, they're in the Barn, right?! And you're the only one small enough to get in and big enough, intelligence-wise, to know what to look for! You can have my steam engine for ten mags. Get my drift now?'

The steam engine! Arvid had seen it many times in Jon's house. It was on a shelf just inside the door to Trond's room and was so shiny and beautiful to look at it almost hurt to think about it. And it worked. Arvid was allowed to have a go one time when Jon and he had been alone, and he had wanted one since he first saw it.

'I haven't used it for years,' Trond said. 'You can have it for ten mags.'

'But which mags do you mean?'

'For Chrissake, of course you know. The ones he uses to paint from. They're in the Barn. Ten of them, you can manage that.'

Arvid knew what Trond meant because he had been to Bandini's once for a glass of water and had seen what was hanging on the walls in there, but he didn't say a word about it to anyone at home.

'All right, I'll see what I can find.'

'Great, come on.'

'No! Not now!' Arvid remembered the dark inside, the place stuffed with darkness, no light from the timber cladding now, no light from the crack in the wall.

'I have to get back in, Dad will be furious. I'll do it after school tomorrow.'

Trond looked at him as he blew smoke from the corner of his mouth and said:

'OK, Death Diver, it's a deal. But don't you mess me about!'

'I won't,' Arvid said.

The day after, he almost ran home from school. On the way he passed the Barn, but he didn't even give it a glance, for he had to hurry home with his bag first and didn't want to think about anything until he had to.

He slung his bag in the hall and shouted to his mother, who was in the kitchen frying meatballs:

'Be right back. Have to go to Jon's to fetch something!' And then he slammed the door before his mother had a chance to answer.

Fatso was sitting on the stoop reading *Arbeiderbladet* as he always did at this time of day. He had his woollen jacket on, it was mid-October and cold, but Fatso didn't take his newspaper inside until the first snow had fallen.

'Hello,' Fatso said. 'How's it going, Arvid?'

Arvid didn't answer, just walked straight by, and as he rounded the corner by Thomassen's Fatso called after him, 'You're as damn polite as your father!'

Arvid walked up the hill to Grevlingveien and sneaked between two houses and down to the Barn from the top. That way not many could see him, for the crack in the wall was on that side, and he was lucky, for no one saw him at all.

He had the knack now, and it was easy to get in through the hole. Instead of wearing a jacket with buttons he had on a thick jumper and he slid in with ease and knelt groping his way forward to find the hole in the floor. And then he found it and pushed himself up with his shoulders hunched, and he was up looking around.

The place was stripped. Not a magazine, not a newspaper, not a comic, not so much as a lousy *Popeye*. Just loads of mess and rubbish and dust, dust and more dust. But beneath the roof sat two men with ropes around their waists and they were up to something, they had hammers and monkey wrenches and they were banging and unscrewing some huge bolts. Arvid stood up fully to see better and then he saw a strip of light widen and then he knew. It was the wall, they were tearing down the wall! Arvid threw himself into the hole like a frightened badger, but he didn't look and halfway down got stuck. He heaved and pulled, but it was no use, his belt was snagged at the back, and he began to take it off as fast as he could. But his fingers were as stiff as dry twigs, and the men were pounding away at the wall making the whole Barn shake, and one shouted to the other:

'All right, Joakim, let it go.' And he gave the wall a savage blow with his hammer. Arvid gasped. Joakim! The wall swayed, he was going to die, he was going to be squashed, and then he screamed:

'Joakim!'

'What?' The man turned. 'Oh, shit me! Olav! There's a kid in here!'

'I was told to say hello!' Arvid yelled.

'What?' The man was desperately banging the wall, striking it again and again, both of them were smashing at it for all they were worth.

'I want to sleep,' Arvid whimpered and buried his head in his armpit. 'I want to sleep.' And then the wall fell, as if in slow motion. Outwards.

'Lord Jesus,' the one called Joakim said as he climbed down. Once he was on the floor he ran over to Arvid, lifted his head off his arm and looked into his face.

'Are you all right, boy?'

Arvid turned round and he could see daylight, and there was his house just across from the Barn. He looked up at Joakim and smiled.

'I thought she was under the floor, but she wasn't. She must have run off somewhere else.'

He struggled to his feet and set off towards the light streaming in where the wall had been, he could see the bright, blue autumn sky and the sun, and then he turned.

'If I wish for a steam engine this Christmas, do you think I'll get one, even if it's expensive?'

'Definitely,' the men said, looking at each other. 'No doubt about it.'

'Great,' Arvid said. 'Bye.' And he ran out of the Barn, his heels banging on the barn wall, that was lying there like a bridge out into the world.

'Jesus,' Joakim said. 'What's the matter with kids nowadays?'

Today You Must Pray to God

One morning the form teacher came in for the first lesson, dropped down heavily on the chair behind his desk, surveyed the class and said:

'Today you must pray to God, for today there may be a nuclear war.' He cleared his throat, took a deep breath and said:

'Nuclear war,' one more time, his double chins shaking, and silence fell on the classroom.

Nuclear war.

Arvid had heard them talking about it at home, and of course he knew what it was. It was the end, for everyone, no joke.

Uncle Rolf had dropped by, and his voice was excited and out of control downstairs in the living room that evening. Uncle Rolf hated the Russians almost as much as he hated farmers, and Arvid had crouched at the top of the stairs, where he would sit when he wanted to listen without being seen, and Dad didn't think the Russians were such bastards, not the way Uncle Rolf did, but he wasn't too cocky either, you could tell from his voice. It didn't cut through the room like Uncle Rolf's did.

Arvid didn't know where Cuba was, it hadn't come up in geography yet, and he didn't know what went on there, but it didn't matter, it was the end anyway, no joke.

After the lesson was over he went home. He unhooked his satchel from the desk, held it under his arm when they walked out for break and slipped quietly and unnoticed through the school gates.

There were four lessons left that day, but he saw no reason to stay at school if there was going to be a nuclear war. If it was all over he would rather wait at home with his mother.

He trudged homewards. He had his high rubber boots on and they were turned down and had Elvis written on the lining, even though it was his mother who liked Elvis, the blue jumper with the zigzag pattern and the cap he always wore, in the summer too sometimes. It was a blue cap with a white stripe along the edge and a white bobble on top, like the ski jumper Toralf Engan wore, and everyone else for that matter, and he used to pull it down over his forehead because it looked tough.

He wasn't frightened, his body was just so suddenly tired that he had to concentrate on every step he took, and the tiredness grew and grew until it lay like lumps beneath his skin, he could almost feel them with his fingers, and his boots were heavy, as if filled with blue clay. He didn't cry because he and his dad had agreed he would not do that so often now, but his face felt as dry as old cardboard and just blinking was an effort of will.

When he got home so early, his mother gave him a puzzled look but said nothing, and he thought that was fine, for when you're about to die there's really nothing to discuss. Even so, it was odd that she was cooking, but then again there was no need to go hungry while you were waiting, so he sat down at the kitchen table, and she gave him two slices of bread with peanut butter and a glass of milk. He said:

'Thanks,' and then he didn't say another word for four days. His body was frozen, he couldn't understand why nothing happened, why no one was concerned, and it took him a long time to thaw, it was as though his body had to be cracked open before things could be as before.

He didn't pray to God, because he didn't believe in God, but he thought that maybe there were others in his class who did. He lay in bed staring at the wall listening to the morning service downstairs in the living room, he heard his dad go to work in the morning and come home in the afternoon, he heard them argue in the kitchen in the evening.

He just lay there and would not get up, and in the end his mother became worried and took him to the doctor although Dad said it was a waste of time. He was a strange doctor, for he didn't look down his throat or listen to his chest or anything, he just talked. But Arvid felt better afterwards even though he was often very tired and could fall asleep in the middle of the day.

Before the War

Above the big radio in the living room hung a photograph of two men in a boxing ring, one of them had just landed a blow on the other, and the one doing the punching was Dad. Arvid stood looking at the picture, the sun was shining at an angle through the blinds making strange patterns on the carpet. It was Saturday morning, and he felt a hand on his shoulder.

'They used to call me Sledge. That was before the war.'

Arvid had heard this so many times, he was fed up with it, but he was not fed up with the photograph. Dad looked so good there above the radio, his body one blur of movement, powerful yet slim, his feet dancing as if they didn't know how to stumble.

Dad held Arvid's shoulder as he studied the picture and said once again:

'That was before the war.'

He spoke a lot about what happened before the war, and once Gry asked kind of casually: 'When was it that you two met, you and Mum?'

'In 1947,' Dad answered trustingly, and Gry went and looked it up in a book and found out what she'd been almost certain about, that 1947 was *after* the war.

'I'm not that fast now,' Dad said.

Maybe not, Arvid thought, but despite being forty-nine he had the body of a fit thirty-year-old. He looked how Arvid would never look, Arvid was certain about that.

Arvid was slight, he didn't look like the others in his family, for he was the only one with dark hair, and he was smaller. He was the smallest in his class and was often roughed up, which was why he would learn to box, his dad had decided, and training had already started. They used the living room as a gym, they moved the table to the side and rolled out a large rug as a boxing ring. They had woollen mittens instead of boxing gloves and they circled round on the rug and his dad punched holes in the air round Arvid's head and lectured:

'Never let them push you around, always give as good as you get, don't put up with anything, it will come back to bite you. And if you have to, hit first, just to set an example.'

And then he shouted insults at Arvid to make him angry. But Arvid didn't get angry, he just felt sad, and one time when he wouldn't hit his dad on the chin although he stuck it out as far as he could, his dad was so annoyed he pushed Arvid in the chest and sent him flying under the sofa. When he refused to come out, his dad got even more annoyed and went into the kitchen cursing and slamming the door and stayed there for a whole hour.

'You're quick on your feet, it's not that,' Dad said, 'but you're too light. You don't have the weight behind your fists. But it will come. Perhaps. Shall we have one more round?'

Dad swung Arvid round, raised his fists and began to dance round the floor. Arvid raised his hands mechanically, without enthusiasm, and they were heavy as lead and he felt empty inside.

'Stop that nonsense, Frank. Leave the boy in peace!' Mum dropped Dad's huge rucksack onto the floor and snapped, 'Here's your stuff. It's time you left. Are you ready, Arvid?'

He was: warm clothes, boots, the Huckleberry Finn book, fishing tackle. He had packed it all before he went to bed.

Uncle Rolf and Dad were going to the cabin by the Bunne Fjord and Arvid was going with them. At first Dad wasn't too pleased about it, but Mum's voice was frosty and clear:

'Arvid is going with you, he needs to get away for a bit and it won't kill you, Frank!' And Dad had to agree that Arvid could use some wind in his hair and a mackerel or two on the hook. The boy was getting slack.

It was still early, the sun was up, the sky blue, and he liked to walk behind Dad and see his broad back carrying the rucksack as far up the hill as Trondhjemsveien to catch the bus to town. The air was cold and fresh and Mum ruffled his hair as they said goodbye at the door and pulled his blue woolly cap down over his ears.

It would be good to go fishing, it would be good to see Dad and Uncle Rolf do their work, it would be good to sit on the bus, for he liked riding on the bus, and it arrived almost immediately and was yellow with green stripes, and the sun gleamed on its shiny windows, and behind it was a long trail of white exhaust fumes.

There was standing room only, and Arvid was allowed to sit on the engine casing and talk to the driver, whom he knew from before, and the driver spoke to him as though he were a grown-up and also asked him about all kinds of things and laughed and joked, and his voice circled round Arvid's head like a gentle cloud. The shuddering of the engine shook his body in a pleasant way, and he felt light and good.

They passed Linderud Manor and Bjerke Trotting Stadium and Aker Hospital, where he was born, and crossed the Sinsen intersection on their way downhill towards Carl Berners Square, where the trolley buses ran. At Carl Berners a lot of passengers got off to change to the tram or another bus and then Arvid had to sit on one of the free seats, but it didn't matter now, and he sat down beside his dad.

'I'm sure the fish will bite today. Perhaps at long last we should give the canoe a run-out? That would be great, wouldn't it?'

Every time they went to the cabin Dad said the same thing, and Arvid knew that nothing would come of it. It never did. But that didn't matter, they could fish from one of the rocks by the shore.

Uncle Rolf had a rowing boat, but Dad didn't want to use it, he didn't need it because in his opinion the canoe belonged to him. Uncle Rolf did not agree. It had been handed down to both of them, he said, and then Dad got angry and would not use the canoe either, so it just lay there.

Sometimes Arvid went in the rowing boat, and Uncle Rolf liked that, for then he could teach Arvid how to talk to the fish to make them bite. Come on then, Jakob, he said, come on, but more often than not Arvid fished from the shore so his dad would not give him that Judas look.

The sun was high and beginning to warm the air as they left the bus in Storgata by Ankertorget and caught the one for Bekkensten. Arvid sat on the long seat at the back, and off they went. At Mosseveien Uncle Rolf was waiting at the stop there, he too had a rucksack, the fishing rod was sticking up from one side and Arvid saw him flag down the bus. As he boarded he gave him his broadest smile.

'Hi, Arvid, you're up and not crying? That's good. Today we're gonna get ourselves a few mackerel.'

'Sure,' Arvid said.

The grown-ups sat together to talk about the job they were going to do, the concrete steps on the path down to the jetty were falling apart, so they had to be fixed, and that was the sort of thing Dad liked to busy himself with. He explained to Uncle Rolf how it should be done and Uncle Rolf nodded and looked at Dad and then glanced out of the window at the Oslo Fjord, calm and shining in the autumn sun, and he probably didn't hear half of it.

Arvid leaned his head back against the rear window and let the vibrations run through his body, tickle his ears, and he closed his eyes and fell asleep.

He was dreaming when his dad stroked his hair and pinched his nose a little to wake him up. He opened his eyes and looked into his dad's teasing smile. At first he couldn't tell who he was and he panicked, but then he sighed with relief and smiled and they had reached Bekkensten and had to get out. They left the bus and it turned up the hill towards Svartskog and they began to walk up to the cabin. It was off the road beyond two large gateposts that Dad had set in before the war, the old hinges screaming as they opened the gate and went into the drive past the flagpole.

They were standing at the top of the steps and Dad was about to unlock the door when it just glided open of its own accord and there was no lock at all, the door had been forced and Dad pushed it carefully. Inside the porch there was a mess, one chair was smashed, the table was upside down, and in the living room all the dresser drawers were pulled out and the contents strewn across the floor.

'Fucking farmers!' Uncle Rolf shouted and ran round picking things off the floor and dropping them again, and Dad asked what the hell farmers had to do with anything and if he shouldn't curse the Russians as well, but he was just as angry as Uncle Rolf, Arvid could see by his face, his jaws were so taut he seemed younger than he was. And when they saw that the one who had been there unannounced had done his business in a corner of the living room he started kicking the staircase to the first floor. He kicked and kicked without saying a word, just whacking one foot against the stairs until the paint started to come off in big flakes. Then he stopped and began to clear up without another word. Arvid and Uncle Rolf helped, and after half an hour's work it didn't look too bad.

Uncle Rolf made some coffee, and cocoa for Arvid, they took out their packed lunches and sat at the table in the porch eating. Dad had to sit on a stool because the other chair had been smashed into kindling. When they had finished, Dad went out into the shed and found all the things they needed to patch up the steps.

Arvid went to greet the sea, he had his high boots on and he waded in the shallow water picking mussels, there were lots of them, until his fingers were blue. He tried skimming stones across the water instead, but even that didn't go so well. He blew on his fingers and held them against his stomach under his jumper. His stomach was smooth and firm and warm, and he shuddered as his cold hands met his skin.

He went back up. The canoe lay on two stands under a spruce tree, and had been there since Granddad died. He ran his finger along the side. The red paint was peeling and when he pressed hard his finger sank into the woodwork. It was a creepy feeling.

Further up the steep hill he heard his dad and Uncle Rolf arguing. Mostly it was his dad's voice he heard. He was on his knees with a bricklayer's trowel, Uncle Rolf was standing beside him with a bucket of cement, looking forlorn. Uncle Rolf wasn't very practical, he preferred to talk. Most of the time this was fine, for Dad loved to work with his hands, but now he was in a bad mood and said:

'You're not much use, you never have been. I remember before the war when we were putting up this whole mess, you weren't much use then either. The old man and I had to do just about everything alone. You always had to be helped. Jesus, I even had to fight your fights at school!'

Uncle Rolf said nothing, and Arvid passed them on the way up to the cabin. He went into the living room and unpacked the fishing tackle from his rucksack, assembled the fishing rod, fixed the line and spinner, put on a warm jacket and went back out. Dad and Uncle Rolf were coming up. Arvid met them on the steps.

'Where are you going?' Dad asked.

'Aren't we going fishing now?'

Dad looked at his watch. 'It's too late. Perhaps we'll have time tomorrow. We'll see.'

Arvid turned, went in, dismantled the rod, stuffed the two parts into the bag and put everything back in the rucksack. He took out *Huckleberry Finn* and sat on the divan and began to read. It was the third time he had read it. It was the finest book ever written and he knew he would read it many more times. He only had to wait a few weeks until the next time, then the desire would return, but now it wasn't easy to concentrate. He kept looking up at his dad, who had been to the well and fetched a bucket of water. Dad always washed with ice-cold water when he was at the cabin, and he tried to make Arvid do the same, but Arvid turned blue all over and had started to refuse.

'Cold water toughens you up,' Dad said. 'You have to harden yourself, if you don't want to be a sissy. When I was young, before the war, I always had a shiver bath in the morning. It helped me endure most things.'

Arvid looked at his dad bent over the bucket, he had filled a pitcher and poured the water over the back of his neck, and it ran down his shoulders, and he stood without moving or

110

shivering and Arvid realised that it was true. He could endure most things.

And suddenly he was as gentle as butter again.

'Would you like something to drink, Arvid?' he asked, taking a bottle of Asina from his rucksack. Asina was good, it tasted like Solo lemonade, but Asina was cheaper. Dad poured a glass and set the bottle and the glass on the table the way they did in cafés. Another bottle was produced from the rucksack, and Arvid knew what it was, it was aquavit. Dad smacked the bottle down on the table.

'Now we grown-ups will have ourselves a dram, for this has been one shit day!' Uncle Rolf fetched two glasses and poured and then they had a shot each and began to talk about the old days, and Arvid sat on the divan reading *Huckleberry Finn* and drinking Asina. He had come to the part where Huck and Jim are on the shipwrecked boat and run into a gang of robbers and it was exciting, but then he was tired again and had to put the book down and sleep a little.

It was Uncle Rolf's voice that woke him. He glanced over at the table where there was almost nothing left in the bottle, the paraffin lamp was lit and Uncle Rolf was shouting:

'You think you're so damn clever at every-thing, you and the old man were always like that, but none of us ever made anything of ourselves, we're just plain workers. And you think you're so damn tough and strong, but you don't even use your head, you know nothing, you never understood the old man was a bastard!'

'Don't talk like that about my father!'

'He was my father too, but he was still a bas-tard! What do you think it was like for me liv-ing alone in Vålerenga with that quarrelsome character after you and your wife moved out? But you were the golden boy, weren't you? You two and the cabin and the damned canoe and all the things the two of you did.'

'The canoe's mine! He always said I was the one who should have it!'

'OK, have it then, for Christ's sake! Take the crappy old canoe, be my guest!'

Uncle Rolf stared furiously at Dad, and then he grinned and turned to Arvid. He leaned forward, went to prop one elbow on the table but missed, and his head knocked the glass over and the aquavit ran down his trousers, he was drunk as a skunk, but he was still grinning.

'Do you know what, Arvid?' he said. 'Do you know what your father used to say? He said he probably isn't your father at all. Actually it was an Italian plumber calling on your mother one morning while he was at work. Heh, heh.' Uncle Rolf sniggered, and Arvid froze and looked at his dad, who looked back with a dull expression in his eyes, he was just as drunk and he frowned and had to concentrate, and then his face darkened and from out of the blue he planted a straight left on Uncle Rolf's nose. Uncle Rolf fell from his chair onto the floor with a thud, his nose began to bleed at once, but he was still sniggering. Arvid could feel his stomach churning faster and faster, he looked from one to the other, Dad was standing with his fist raised and was about to strike again.

'I am not Italian!' Arvid screamed. 'I'm Norwegian! I speak Norwegian and you're both pissed. Don't you think I know?'

Uncle Rolf peered up at Dad and wiped his nose and there was blood all over his hand.

'Christ, Arvid, I was only joking.'

'Don't joke about that sort of thing, you fat oaf,' Dad said, with a lurch. 'And now you're going to get a beating like you haven't had since before the war!' And with that he went at Uncle Rolf, and Uncle Rolf was scared and said:

'Are you out of your mind?'

Dad looked dangerous, with his shoulders raised and fists clenched in front of him and his chin stuck out like a knife. Arvid took aim and punched that chin for all he was worth, and his dad snapped back and shook his head and turned, but Arvid was running up the stairs to the first floor. He heard a thud from below, and he crawled under a bed.

'You're out of your mind!' Uncle Rolf shouted again, and then something was knocked over in the living room, the front door slammed and Arvid heard the heavy footsteps across the drive and the hinges of the gate screeching as it was thrust open.

'Arvid!' Dad shouted from the living room, but Arvid did not answer, he just huddled up against the wall.

'Dammit,' Dad said. 'Dammit!' And it sounded as if he were crying, but he couldn't have been, and anyway it was difficult to tell when you were under a bed on the first floor.

The aquavit bottle clinked and the front door slammed again and there was total silence. Arvid crept out from under the bed and went to the stairs and listened. He tiptoed halfway down and looked around the sitting room. The bottle was lying empty on the table and the room was deserted. He went all the way down. There was no one in the cabin any more, he was alone. The front door was ajar and he went out onto the steps. It was pitch black now, it was night, there was forest around the cabin on all sides and it bore down on the walls.

'Dad,' he shouted, but it wasn't much of a shout, he could barely hear it himself, and no one answered. Then there was a proper shout from the jetty. It was his dad's voice, but it did not sound as it usually did, it was high-pitched and piercing, and Arvid ran down between the trees that stood like a wall and wanted to block his path, but he didn't pay them any heed, he just ran in the darkness, down, down. The roots criss-crossing the path knocked against his feet, but he managed to stay upright, he didn't want to stumble and so he didn't. He took the concrete steps in great leaps and bounds, and he was good at jumping, he flew through the autumn night panting for breath, but it was not he who was panting, the panting was driving *him*, in heavy rasping gasps, and he could hear them from a distance as though they were not his, and once he had to turn and look back, but he was alone.

'Dad!' he shouted. 'Where are you?' No one answered, but then he heard his dad cursing and then there was a loud splash.

Arvid raced all the way down, his legs flashing like drumsticks while his gaze scanned the shore searching for something that was not as it should be, but at night nothing is as it should be, he ought to have known, and then he was on the jetty and just managed to stop before he fell head first into the water. On the edge of the jetty was a paddle and a few metres into the fjord was the canoe, upside down. There was a big hole at one end, and the jagged edges sticking up were brown and rotten, and suddenly everything was silent, the night and the forest behind him, the glistening fjord.

A roar splintered the silence and a face broke the surface right in front of Arvid. He jumped back and it felt like a cold finger scraping down his spine, he covered his eyes, for he thought it might be a water sprite, but it wasn't, it was his dad, and he was roaring:

'Jesus! The damned tub's rotten to the core! I stepped right through it!'

Arvid jumped down into the water and waded a few metres and grabbed Dad's one hand and pulled and tugged so hard his arm almost came off, and Dad crawled and spat and at last he was up. But then he slipped on the seaweed, for it was low tide, and they both fell, and Dad landed with his head in Arvid's lap. Arvid could feel the weight on his thigh, and he held the head tight. He was trembling with cold now, for he was wet up to his waist, and then he saw for the first time that Dad was turning bald. He stroked the thinning wet hair and said:

'Shhh, Dad, it will be fine, everything'll be fine, right?' Dad turned his head up to look at him and then he was sick, it gushed from his mouth and down Arvid's legs.

'It's OK, Dad,' Arvid said.

Dad spat in despair and said:

'This would never have happened before the war.'

'I know,' Arvid said. 'I know.'